Du Iz Tak?

Carson Ellis

CANDLEWICK PRESS

Du iz tak?

Ma nazoot.

Ta ta!

Ru badda unk ribble.

Su.

Bore inkin Icky.

Icky, ru badda unk ribble.

Unk ribble!

RUP FURT!

VOOBECK!

BOOBY VOOBECK!

Rup furt.

Su!

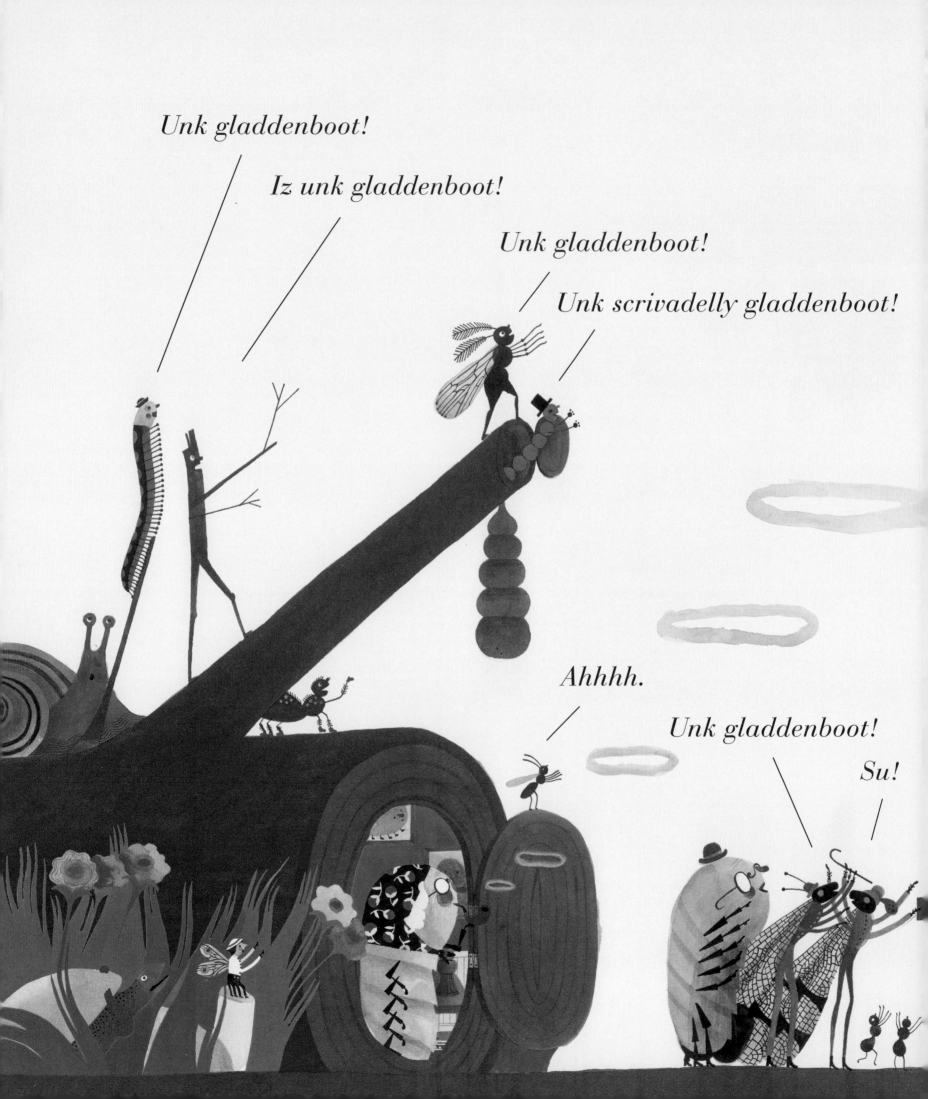

Iz tak unk gladdenboot?

Unk gladdenboot!

Ta ta, oodas!

Ta ta, Icky.
Ta ta, Ooky.

Ta ta, furt.

Du iz tak?

For the good folks of the KBK

First edition 2016

Library of Congress Catalog Card Number 2015934273
ISBN 978-0-7636-6530-2

16 17 18 19 20 21 APS 10 9 8 7 6 5 4 3 2 1

Printed in Humen, Dongguan, China

FSC
www.fsc.org

MIX
Paper from responsible sources
FSC® C101537

This book was typeset in Bauer Bodoni.
The illustrations were done in gouache and ink.

Candlewick Press
99 Dover Street
Somerville, Massachusetts 02144

visit us at www.candlewick.com

Ta ta!